BY **JANE CLARKE**   ILLUSTRATED BY **JAMES BROWN**

LOTTIE L♥VES NATURE

Hedgehog Surprise

 FIVE QUILLS

 HI!

My name is Lottie and I love nature!

♡ LOTTIE ♡

When I grow up,
I am going to be a
wildlife show presenter
like Samira Breeze
who presents
Every Little Thing.

EVERY
LITTLE THING
MATTERS

People are part of nature.
If nature thrives so do we!

I am keeping notes about lots
of cool stuff about nature,
wildlife and the Earth.

EVERY LITTLE THING MATTERS!

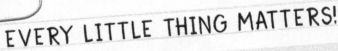

MY PETS

Did you know that a fully-grown macaw can weigh as much as a cat?

Did you know dogs are descended from wolves?

EINSTEIN

NACHO

♡ ≷ NATURE NOTE ≶ ♡

There are hundreds of different types of parrots, including budgerigars. Parrots love to mimic people, and imitate noises. They can live as long as humans.

I live with my mum and my twin brother Al. He hates spiders, but loves Science!

To the Awesome Andersons, with love and thanks! – JC

For Madison and Jude, who love being outside! – JB

LOTTIE LOVES NATURE: HEDGEHOG SURPRISE

First published in Great Britain in 2022 by Five Quills
93 Oakwood Court, London W14 8JZ

www.fivequills.co.uk

Five Quills and associated logos are a trademark of Five Quills Ltd.

Text copyright © Jane Clarke 2022
Illustrations copyright © Five Quills 2022

Edited by Natascha Biebow at Blue Elephant Storyshaping
Designed by Amy Cooper

A CIP record for this title is available from the British Library

ISBN 978 1 912923 10 6

1 3 5 7 9 10 8 6 4 2

Printed and bound in Great Britain by Clays Ltd, Elcograf S.p.A.

MIX
Paper from
responsible sources
FSC® C018072
FSC
www.fsc.org

CONTENTS

Marvellous Moths

Lottie Boffin was watching her favourite wildlife show, 'Every Little Thing'. She wanted to be a wildlife presenter just like Samira Breeze when she grew up!

"Discover the creatures that visit your garden when it gets dark," Samira was saying. "If you make a moth box, you'll see lots of marvellous moths — and while you're outside, you might be lucky enough to spot an owl, a bat, or even a hedgehog. Don't forget to send in your nature notes for a chance to win our amazing prize, and remember: every little thing matters!"

Lottie tingled with excitement. It was her dream to win the chance to be on the show with Samira. Her nature notebook was almost ready to send in. A few pages on night-time creatures would finish it off nicely.

There was no time to lose. It would soon be dark outside. Lottie jumped to her feet, startling the parrot dozing on her shoulder. Nacho let out a loud

ZZZZZ

squawk and flew to his perch.
Lottie smiled as he sleepily
shuffled his feathers and closed
his eyes. She had inherited the parrot
from her Great Aunt Pru, and now he
was a much-loved part of their family.

Even Einstein, their dog, had stopped barking when he squawked. Well, most of the time, anyway.

"Cardboard box, egg box, sticky tape . . ." Lottie raced around the house collecting what she needed to make a moth box. There was one thing missing. "Al," Lottie yelled, "can I use your torch?"

Lottie's twin brother was in his bedroom, shining his torch down the hose of the vacuum cleaner. "Sorry," he said. "I've been

4

experimenting with sucking power, in case my time machine gets pulled into a black hole. I need my torch to see where the blockage is. I have to get it out before Mum asks why I broke the vacuum cleaner."

"Never mind," said Lottie, "your secret's safe with me." She glanced out of the window. "Noah's in his garden. I'll ask him."

She dashed outside and stood on the plant pot next to the Parfitts' fence. Noah Parfitt was gazing up into the sky. "What are you up to?" she asked.

"Working out the position of Mars," he said.

Lottie wasn't surprised. Noah was obsessed with Mars. It was Noah's ambition to be one of the first human beings to live there.

"We should be able to see Mars when the sky gets a bit darker," Noah went on.

"I'd rather see moths," Lottie told him. "Samira says they're really important pollinators. Moths and their caterpillars are also a great food source for lots of other creatures, including birds and bats and hedgehogs. I want to set up a moth box so I can take a closer look at some. But moths fly towards light, and Al's using his torch. Can you help?"

"I'll find a torch and bring it round."

Noah grinned. "Dad hates moths. He says it's because they make holes in his golf jumpers and Petunia tells him off."

Lottie giggled. All Mr Parfitt ever thought about was golf. He'd turned the whole of his back garden into a golf course, complete with artificial grass and flags!

"You only find clothes moths in a house," she told Noah. "I'm more interested in the sorts of moths that live outside. I'll make the moth box while you find a torch."

Lottie went back into the kitchen and taped the opened egg box inside the cardboard box. Then she let two of the top flaps drop down at an angle for moths to get in.

In no time at all, Noah appeared, waving a torch. He stared at what Lottie had done with the box. "What's the egg box for?" he asked.

"It's so the moths have something to rest on when they're inside the big box," Lottie explained. "Let's set it up. It's almost dusk." Einstein sniffed curiously at the box as she carried it outside.

Their feet rustled through the fallen leaves in the Boffins' garden. "Dad doesn't like autumn," Noah commented. "He hates picking fallen leaves out of his golf holes."

"I love autumn!" Lottie happily kicked up the leaves as she carried the box past the birdbath, the bug hotel and the little container pond they had made.

"It needs to go in a dark spot, like this," she told Noah. "Otherwise the moths get confused by the light coming from the house."

⋛ MOTH WATCH ⋚

Moths love light! To look at them more closely, I made a moth box.

I opened the egg box and taped the flat sides to the bottom of a big cardboard box. This is to give the moths something to rest on.

I pushed down the flaps of the big box to make slopes.

I turned on the torch and put it next to the egg box. Then I went away and left the box for 30 minutes. Lots of moths came!

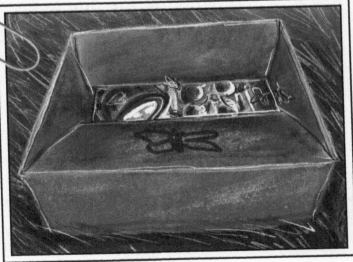

  ⚠️ NOTE: Be sure to release the moths later!

Lottie switched on the torch and put it in the box. "Now we just have to wait for a bit," she said.

Noah peered up into the darkening

sky. "The stars will be coming out soon. Planet Mars looks like a star in the night sky. It glows red because of the dust." He sighed. "I can't wait to go there!"

The **Sun** is a star. All the planets orbit around the Sun. Most stars have planets orbiting around them!

Mars - We could live here with the help of technology. We could extract water from ice, it's not too hot or too cold, and there is some gravity, like on Earth.

Mercury and **Venus** - Far too hot to live on ...

Earth is unique! It's the only known planet that has liquid water on the surface and intelligent life.

Mars is our next-door neighbour planet in our solar system. So that intergalactic post can reach me on Mars, after my address, I'll need to add: Mars, The Solar System, The Milky Way, The Virgo Cluster, The Universe.

A galaxy is a group of solar systems. Our solar system is in the Milky Way galaxy, which is part of the Virgo Cluster. There are billions of galaxies in the Universe and trillions of billions of planets. Scientists are searching for signs of other life in Space.

Jupiter and **Saturn** — Made mostly of gas! Living here would be like always being on a very cold cloud.

Uranus and **Neptune**. These ice giants are far too cold for people!

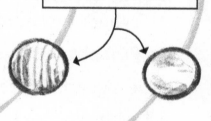

What kind of music do you hear in Space?

A Neptune.

"Well, I'm staying here and looking after Earth," said Lottie. "They say it looks a beautiful blue from Space, because of all the oceans . . . "

Woof! Einstein barked, making Lottie and Noah jump. His ears pricked up and he raced to the back gate.

Woof woof woof!

"What's he heard?" asked Noah.

"Probably just the Goods' cat." Lottie sighed. Einstein was getting on well with Nacho, but he still couldn't resist chasing their other neighbours' cat, Precious. "I'd better grab him before Mrs Good tells us off!"

Lottie ran to the gate. Einstein had stopped barking. His head was tilted to one side as he listened intently to something. Lottie listened too. Something was scuffling outside the gate. "That's not Precious," she murmured, as Einstein snuffled at the bottom of the gate and backed away.

"What is it?" asked Noah.

"There's only one way to find out." Lottie slowly opened the gate.

2

Prickly Visitor

A cute little creature with a pointed nose, button eyes and a back full of spines pattered into the back garden.

"Wow! It's a hedgehog!" Lottie's heart leapt with joy as she pulled Einstein out of its way. It was a lovely surprise. She hadn't expected to be lucky enough to see one.

"They're getting quite rare," she

told Noah. "It's really important to help them to survive in the wild."

The hedgehog snuffled around their feet.

"What's it doing?" asked Noah.

"Probably looking for something to eat," Lottie said. "Hedgehogs travel a long way every night looking for food like moths and worms and slugs. In the autumn, they need to eat a lot and put on weight to see them through the winter."

PRICKLY NEIGHBOURS

There are 17 species of hedgehogs in the wild.
They live in Africa, Asia, Europe and New Zealand.

Newborn hedgehogs are born with white spines under their skin. By the time they are adults, they have 5,000–10,000 spines made of keratin, just like our fingernails.

When hedgehogs are around 8 weeks old, they go off to live on their own. They have good hearing and a sharp sense of smell, but bad eyesight.

When they are afraid, hedgehogs curl up in a ball – good if the danger is a fox, but bad if they are crossing a road and a car is coming!

HEDGEHOG NEST

Hedgehogs are nocturnal, so they come out after dark to sniff out their food. They love to eat slugs, worms, caterpillars, beetles, earwigs and moths.

Hedgehogs build cosy day nests out of leaves and twigs or fallen branches. I made a hedgehog shelter in my garden out of an old wooden crate and lots of leaves.

Be sure to check under a bonfire before you light it in case it's a hedgehog home!

Hedgehogs hibernate in the winter (see p. 46-47).

EVERY LITTLE THING MATTERS

NOTE: A hedgehog out during the day might be in trouble, or sick. Contact the nearest wildlife rescue centre if you think it needs rescuing!

"Let's get it a saucer of milk," suggested Noah.

"Samira says people used to do that a lot," Lottie said thoughtfully, "but now we know milk upsets their tummies. The best thing for them to drink is water. They can also have a bit of dog or cat food that doesn't contain any fish. Here, hang on to Einstein's collar while I find some."

Lottie nipped into the kitchen and came out holding a saucer of Einstein's dog food. Einstein wagged his tail and drooled as Lottie put it down on the ground.

The hedgehog sniffed the air, then pottered up to it and began to nibble.

Noah held tightly onto Einstein. **WOOF!** Einstein's bark was clearly a complaint. **WOO-OOF!**

The hedgehog stopped eating and scurried towards the shadows at the back of the garden. Einstein pulled Noah towards the saucer and gobbled up the remains of the dog food.

"He's too strong for me," Noah laughed, letting go of the dog.

The back gate creaked.

"Uh-oh, Mrs Good's come to complain abut the barking," Lottie said.

"No, it's just my dad!" Noah said.

Mr Parfitt shone a tiny torch at them. A moth suddenly swirled around the beam light. "Eek!" Mr Parfitt yelled, swatting it away. "Have you seen the big torch?" he asked. "I just switched on the outside lights and they blew a fuse. I need a proper torch to see what I'm doing."

"We're using it to attract moths into a box," Lottie confessed.

"Ugh, moths!" Mr Parfitt shuddered.

"Please could we swap torches?" Lottie suggested. "A tiny bit of light will be enough for the moths."

"I suppose so . . ." Noah's dad

reluctantly disentangled the tiny torch from his keyring and handed it to Lottie.

Lottie carefully put her hand in the moth box and swapped the torches. She could feel soft wings flutter against her skin. "Wow! There are a lot of moths in here already," she said with a smile. She peered in the box. "Most of them are quite small, but there are a couple of really big ones!"

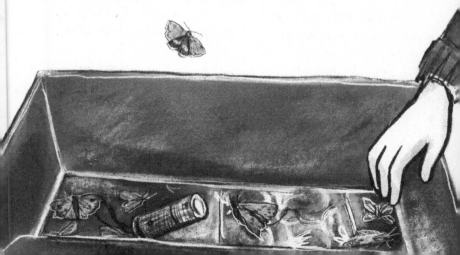

MOTH OR BUTTERFLY?

Most moths only fly at night, though some do come out during the day. Butterflies are active during the daytime.

Most moths have dark, shadowy patterns on their wings, so they can hide from hungry predators. This is called camouflage. A few do have coloured wings like butterflies do.

Most moths rest with their wings down.

Most butterflies rest with their wings up.

Moth antennae – furry or feathery edges.

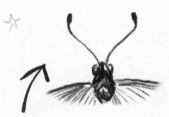

Butterfly antennae – thin with a bulb at the end.

MARVELLOUS MOTHS

Moths are important pollinators. They help transfer pollen from the male to the female parts of flowers so the plant can make fruit and seeds.

Moths are also an important food source for other wildlife, including bats and hedgehogs.

There are thousands of different species of moths, from tiny micro moths to hawk moths that are as big as a hummingbird.

Tiny Micro Moth

Hawk Moth

"Just don't let those moths out while I'm standing here!" Mr Parfitt said nervously.

Noah was looking at the sky again. "Hey, Dad," he said, "turn off the big torch and take a look. There are no clouds tonight. We should be able to spot Mars."

They stared up into the night sky. High above them, a thin line of light streaked across the sky.

"A shooting star!" gasped Lottie.

"The proper name is a meteor," Noah corrected her. "They're small

pieces of rock or dust from a comet or asteroid that burned up as they entered the Earth's atmosphere."

"Cool!" Lottie exclaimed.

"What's the difference between a comet and an asteroid?" Mr Parfitt asked.

"Asteroids are mostly made of rock, and comets are mostly made of ice and dust," Noah said excitedly. "They could be really useful to people when we live on Mars. We could mine them for ice to use for water and fuel!"

"That would be useful," his dad agreed.

NOAH'S NEXT LEVEL:
Asteroids, Meteors and Comets

Asteroids are small, rocky objects that orbit the Sun, but they are smaller than planets. Most of the asteroids orbit within the asteroid belt — a region between the orbits of Mars and Jupiter.

We orbit the Sun, too!

Comets are also small objects that orbit the Sun, mostly made of ice and dust. In Space, astronauts could melt them down for drinking water, and split their oxygen and hydrogen molecules to make fuel and air for breathing.

Meteors are small pieces of rock or dust that enter the Earth's atmosphere from outer Space. Most burn up before they hit the ground. You see them as a streak of light, also known as a shooting star.

We call the pieces that land on Earth meteorites.

What do you call a Space rock made of ham?

A meat-eor.

Mr Parfitt squinted at the night sky. "Now, where's Mars?"

"Look up between those two branches of the apple tree . . ." Noah pointed to a glowing star on the horizon. "You'll see it better if you take a couple of steps to your right . . ."

"Watch out for the hedgehog and the moths—" Lottie squealed.

Too late. Mr Parfitt kicked over the box.

"What was that?" Mr Parfitt clicked on his torch.

A cloud of moths of all sorts of shapes and sizes swirled around the beam of light.

"Yikes! Get away from me!" Mr Parfitt shrieked, hurling the torch onto the grass. He turned and ran back home. "Noah, bring the torches in!" he called over the gate.

Lottie retrieved the big torch. One large moth was still dancing around the light. Its wings were a beautiful patchwork of different shades of brown.

"Perfect camouflage to hide from predators," Lottie murmured, memorising the patterns so she could draw it in her notebook.

"Shame about the moth box," Noah said, looking at the crumpled cardboard. He picked up the little torch.

"That's okay. I was going to let them go, anyway. I'm just glad none of the moths were hurt." Lottie shone the light on the ground and began to collect up all the cardboard.

"Where's the hedgehog?" Noah asked.

"Probably hiding from all the noise," Lottie said. "Come round tomorrow and we'll see if we can find it."

3

The Best Nest

"If the hedgehog's still in the garden, it'll be asleep," Lottie told Noah the next day. "Einstein will sniff it out. I'll keep hold of his collar so he doesn't frighten the hedgehog – or get his nose prickled!"

Einstein snuffled enthusiastically round the garden, stopping at a pile of leaves under the apple tree.

"Sit!" Lottie told him. She dropped to her knees and began to search carefully through the leaves. Einstein put his head to one side and gave a little whine.

Yes! The hedgehog's prickly back appeared between the leaves. Close up, Lottie could see that each stripy brown spike had a lighter tip. The hedgehog was curled up fast asleep. Lottie grinned at Noah and pointed with her fingers to her lips. Quietly, she backed away, dragging Einstein with her.

"Is that the hedgehog's winter nest?" asked Noah.

"No, it's just a place to rest through the day," Lottie said. "It'll need to find a sheltered spot to make a proper nest when the weather gets colder. Hedgehogs hibernate so they don't need to find as much food or use up energy during the winter."

"Hibernation would be very useful for long journeys through Space, too." Noah grinned. "In fact, scientists are studying to see if people can be put into a sort of hibernation. One day, I might travel to Mars in a suspended animation life-support pod."

"Hibernating would make the journey go quickly," Lottie said thoughtfully. "Maybe sleeping through winter makes that seem really short, too."

NOAH'S NEXT LEVEL:
Can We Hibernate?

It takes around seven months to get to Mars, and it'll take even longer if we travel to other planets! People would need less space, water and food if they could travel in hibernation pods.

Scientists wonder if humans might be able to hibernate in the same way that animals like hedgehogs do when the weather gets cold. They think the key is lowering body temperature. People would need to fatten up before travelling, just like animals do.

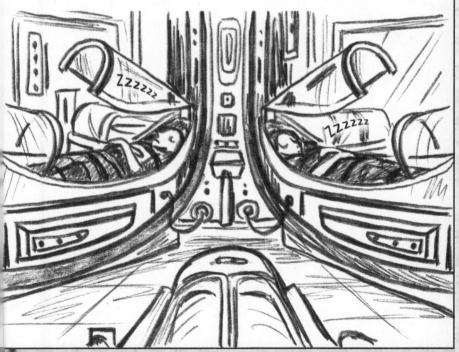

WHO HIBERNATES?

Hibernation is a winter sleep, where body temperature drops, and breathing and heart rate slows.

Many creatures hibernate so they can survive cold, dark winters without having to find food.
Here are some hibernators:

Hedgehogs

Squirrels

Dormice

Bats

Queen Bumblebees

Butterflies and moths

Ladybirds

Tortoises

Bears

Many frogs, toads and newts

Snakes

Chipmunks

Many creatures hibernate for short periods, wake up, eat, then go back to sleep. But bears can sleep for more than 100 days without eating, drinking or wee-ing!

Zzzzzzzz!

"I'd love it if this hedgehog decided to hibernate in my garden!" said Lottie.

"Wouldn't Einstein disturb it?" asked Noah.

"Not if we make it a nice, safe shelter." Lottie grinned. "We could make a hedgehog house out of that small wooden vegetable crate I saw in the garage. It's full of apples that fell off the tree. Come on."

Einstein and Noah followed as Lottie headed for the garage.

Lottie took the bruised apples out of the crate and piled them up on the garage floor.

They rolled everywhere! Einstein tried took a bite out of one and spat it straight out.

ptttthp!

"Maybe we should have asked your mum first," Noah suggested.

"She doesn't like being disturbed when she's busy in the shop," Lottie said confidently. "She won't mind. She told me these apples are only good for making apple sauce."

Lottie examined the empty crate. A couple of the side slats were already loose. She pulled them off. "Perfect," she announced. "The hedgehog can get in under here. We'll fill it full of nice, dry leaves so it can make a bed."

"We can use this, then," Noah

grabbed the leaf rake hanging on the garage wall.

Einstein followed them outside. "Sit and stay!" Lottie told him. "Hedgehogs are too prickly to play with."

"Hola!" Nacho greeted them from his perch on the fence. He was holding out his wings, enjoying the breeze that ruffled his feathers.

"Hola! " Lottie and Noah replied.

Nacho watched curiously as Lottie chose a sheltered spot in the back corner of the garden. Then she laid the crate upside down so the opening was close to the fence.

"The gap between the fence and the entrance has to be big enough for a hedgehog, but too small for Einstein," Lottie explained. "Now, we need to stuff some dry leaves and grass inside. Then we'll heap up leaves on the top of it."

Noah began to rake up the leaves, being careful not to disturb the ones around the hedgehog.

Soon, the crate was entirely hidden under a big pile of leaves.

"This will be the best nest ever for a hedgehog!" Lottie grinned. "Come back when it's totally dark. We can watch out for the hedgehog waking up, and maybe see some other night creatures."

"If it's not too windy," Noah commented, pushing away the hair that had blown into his eyes.

"It's got very breezy," Lottie admitted. "But often the wind drops at night."

Whooosh!

A sudden strong gust of wind swept across the garden. The pile of leaves over the crate swirled and whirled into the air — and so did the ones under the apple tree where the hedgehog was hidden.

The hedgehog scurried towards the back of the garden as the wind blew a big pile of autumn leaves over the fence.

Nacho took to the air with a startled

squawwwwk!

"NO-OOO!" An agonised yell came from next door. Lottie and Noah peered over the fence. Mr Parfitt had leaves all over him – and so did his golf course!

4

Lots of Leaves

Mr Parfitt plucked a leaf out of his hair and glumly surveyed his back garden.

"My golf holes are full of leaves!" he groaned. "They'll have to be cleared out. And I still haven't fixed the outside lights. Petunia's coming round for golf practice this evening and we'll need them to be able to play. I'm never going to get everything ready in time!"

"Don't worry, we'll help clear the leaves," Lottie told him.

"Oh, thank you!" Mr Parfitt breathed a sigh of relief. "I had to order new lights, and I need to go and collect them now. Noah, don't use that leaf rake! It'll damage the artificial grass."

"Then we'll have to pick up every

single one by hand!" Noah grumbled.

"It's okay, we need them for the hedgehog shelter." Lottie fetched the washing-up bowl from her kitchen and joined Noah again in the Parfitts' garden to pick up the leaves.

"Some of these are just beautiful!" Lottie held up a perfect orangy-yellow leaf. The light shone through it, showing a network of veins. "They're from all sorts of different trees," Lottie went on, "not just the apple tree. They must have blown in from other gardens. I'll keep some to stick in my notebook."

TERRIFIC TREES

Evergreen trees keep their green needle-like leaves all year.

Deciduous trees have big, flat leaves that drop in the autumn.

CLEVER LEAVES

The leaves' job is to turn sunlight into sugar food for the tree. This is called photosynthesis. In the autumn, when there is less sunlight, the tree stores all the food the leaves have made in the stems and roots, and the leaves drop to the ground.

When the temperature warms up in spring, the tree starts to grow new leaves.

AUTUMN

SPRING

FABULOUS LEAVES

Each tree has a distinctive leaf shape.

HORSE CHESTNUT

SYCAMORE

ASH

OAK

HOLLY

FIELD MAPLE

BEECH

HAWTHORNE

HAZEL

Nacho watched from the fence as they picked up the last of the leaves and returned with them to the Boffins' garden.

WOOF! WOOF WOOF! Einstein barked when they opened the gate. He stood well back and stared suspiciously at them.

Lottie tipped the leaves out over the little hedgehog shelter.

"Now, what can we lay over the top to make sure the leaves don't blow away again?" Lottie wondered.

"This!" Noah picked up a twiggy fallen branch from under the apple tree.

Woof! Einstein leapt up and

snatched the end. Noah dragged the dog and the branch towards the hedgehog lodge.

"It's not a game!" Noah gasped.

"Einstein thinks it is," Lottie giggled. She picked up his ball from the lawn. "Hey, Einstein," she called. "Leave the stick alone. Fetch!" She tossed the ball and Einstein bounded after it.

He dropped it at her feet and looked up at her hopefully. Lottie glanced over to Noah. He was still wrestling the stick into position. She picked up the slobbery ball and threw it again – and again.

"Done!" Noah announced.

"Be back in a minute," Lottie called. "I have to wash my hands!" She headed towards the kitchen, and returned holding out a banana.

"Want to share?" she asked Noah.

"No, thanks," said Noah, "but I think Nacho does!"

Nacho was bobbing his head up and down expectantly. Lottie broke off a piece of the banana and held it up for him to take.

"Now, what else can we do to make the garden more hedgehog friendly?" Lottie asked.

"It already looks like a great place for a hedgehog," Noah said. "It's got somewhere to drink." He pointed to the little pond that he and Lottie had made.

"And it's safe because we put some rocks on the side so that small creatures can climb out," Lottie added.

Pond

Noah grinned and pointed to

the bug hotel. "We already made a hedgehog restaurant . . ."

Lottie finished the banana and went over to it. She peered into its nooks and crannies. Several slugs and snails were living on the bottom layer.

"The hedgehog will find some food here," she said, thoughtfully. "But I can't see any worms and they love those. Samira says you get lots of worms in a compost heap. I've been meaning to make one for ages. I'll start with this banana skin." She took it to a spot by the back fence and dropped it onto the ground.

SQUAWK! Nacho swooshed down and nabbed it. He circled into the air.

"Hey!" Lottie shouted as Nacho flew off with his prize.

"Will he come back?" Noah asked worriedly.

SQUAWK!

"Oh, yes," said Lottie, "he won't go far from his home territory." She thought for a moment. "Not like hedgehogs. Samira says they like to travel miles a night in search of food."

"But when the gate's shut, it's stuck in your garden," Noah pointed out.

"There are no gaps in the fences between the gardens, or at the back, are there?"

"No! We have to fix that before your dad gets back." Lottie dashed off to get a garden trowel.

Lottie dug a small hole under her back fence, then carefully gouged out another one beneath the fence on the Goods' side.

"Yes!" she grinned. "Hedgehogs have

to be able to roam around at night," Lottie said. "The Goods will never notice, and nor will your dad."

Lottie crossed to the other side of her garden and quickly and quietly dug a small opening under the fence between her garden and Noah's.

"Here." She handed Noah the trowel. "There's nothing natural in your garden, so the hedgehog won't stop long. Make a small opening on the other side of the fence in your garden so it can go through."

"I'll have to do it secretly later," Noah said. "Dad's back with his new lights."

"Nacho's back too." Lottie smiled as her parrot settled back on his favourite place on the fence. "I wonder what happened to the banana skin?"

5

Brilliant Bats

Lottie and Noah balanced on a flowerpot and peered over the fence. Mr Parfitt and Petunia's golf session was in full swing. It was as bright as day in the Parfitts' garden thanks to the new outside lights. A big moth fluttered around them.

"Those lights will confuse the wildlife," murmured Lottie.

"They won't be able to tell night from day."

"It's much darker in your garden," Noah agreed. "Let's go and look for the hedgehog again."

"It'll take our eyes a while to get used to the dark." Lottie and Noah stared into the shadows at the back of the Boffins' garden. On Lottie's shoulder, Nacho sleepily turned his head and buried his beak between his feathers.

Somewhere in the distance an owl hooted. **HOOO-HOOO-OOO!**

Nacho startled awake and dug his claws into Lottie's shoulder.

"That put me off my swing!" Mr Parfitt complained loudly from next door.

"Wish we could see it." Lottie scratched Nacho's head. "I've heard quite a few owls, but I've never seen one in the wild." Nacho's eyes were closing sleepily.

"It's parrot bedtime," she giggled.

"But hedgehog wake-up time – look!" Noah pointed to a spot under the apple tree. The hedgehog was snuffling contentedly in the leaves.

As they watched, a small winged

shadow swooped over the tree. Lottie stifled a squeal of delight.

"That's a bat!" she whispered happily. The shadow whirled above them. "It's probably hunting moths! Our ears can't hear them, but if we had a bat detector, we'd be able to make out clicks and squeaks."

"Bats are cool. They find things using sound waves," said Noah. "The sounds bounce off things and echo back to the bat, so they can locate them. Ultrasound and echolocation will be very useful on Mars!"

BRILLIANT BATS

Bats are the only mammal that truly flies. Their wings are their arm bones with spread out fingers, covered in a skin membrane. They live in all parts of the world except the Arctic and Antarctica.

Bat

The smallest is the Kitti's hog-nosed bat (also called the bumblebee bat).

Flying fox

Kitti's hog-nosed bat

The largest is the golden-capped fruit bat (also called the flying fox).

Most bats are nocturnal. In the daytime, they roost upside down in caves, hollow trees and buildings. They eat mostly insects, but some are vegetarian. Only vampire bats drink blood!

Each species of bat has a different language of squeaks, squawks, clicks and cackles. These sound waves, called ultrasound, are too high-pitched for people to hear.

Bats have very good hearing. When they're flying around in the dark, they make ultrasonic clicks. The clicks echo off objects (like trees, but also food, like insects). The bat's brain then works out how far away it is from the objects. This is called echolocation or biosonar. Bats, whales and dolphins also use it to help navigate and find food.

NOAH'S NEXT LEVEL:
Echolocation

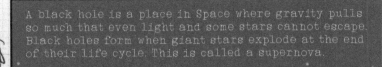

A black hole is a place in Space where gravity pulls so much that even light and some stars cannot escape. Black holes form when giant stars explode at the end of their life cycle. This is called a supernova.

SUPERNOVA

> Just like bats, scientists use echolocation to find black holes. That'll be very important if we ever travel between solar systems!

Scientists believe there is probably a black hole somewhere in our galaxy (the Milky Way), but don't worry — it is many, many light years away from Earth.

Space is mind-bogglingly big! A light year is how far light travels in one Earth Year. One light year is around 9.5 trillion km (6 trillion miles).

> I'm 26,000 light years from the centre of the Milky Way galaxy!

The bat disappeared into the night sky. "Where's the hedgehog gone?" Lottie peered into the darkness.

"Uh-oh!" Noah pointed to the bottom of the fence. A prickly back was disappearing through the hole into the Parfitts' garden. "I didn't think it would roam around when they were playing golf," he groaned. "Dad will freak out!"

"The hedgehog might get hit by a golf ball!" Lottie gasped. "Come on, we have to save it!" Nacho clung onto her shoulder as they ran round next door.

6

Slugs and Surprises

"Hola!" Nacho greeted Mr Parfitt and Petunia.

"Shhhh!" Noah's dad told them. "I'm neck and neck with Petunia and I need to concentrate on this final hole so I can win!"

He raised his club and aimed towards the hole closest to the Boffins' side of his garden.

"Pete, wait!" Petunia shrieked. "Look, there's a hedgehog in that hole!"

Noah's dad dropped his golf club in surprise. Petunia raced up to the golf hole, closely followed by Lottie and Noah.

"Awww," Petunia gurgled. "It's curled up into a little ball."

"Hedgehogs curl up when they're frightened," Lottie said anxiously. "Is it okay?" She got down on her knees to take a closer look, but all she could see were its spikes.

"Where on earth did it come from?" Mr Parfitt asked, mystified.

"That little gap, under the fence," Noah said, pointing it out.

"I'll block that up right now!" Mr Parfitt declared.

"Please don't," Lottie pleaded. "I've made it a home in my garden, but hedgehogs need to be able to roam."

"Oh, do let it roam into your garden, Pete," Petunia said. "Hedgehogs are so-ooo cute."

"But they have fleas, don't they?" Mr Parfitt objected.

"Not very often," Lottie corrected him.

"Even so, I can't have a hedgehog

in a golf hole!" Mr Parfitt knelt down
and gingerly tried to pick up the
hedgehog with his hand that was
wearing a golf glove.

"It's no good," he said. "It seems
to have wedged itself in."

He stood back up. "I don't want to get prickled, or catch fleas," he said.

"Or frighten it more," Lottie added. "I think we should lure it out with some tasty slugs."

"Ew, slugs!" Petunia shuddered. She looked round Mr Parfitt's perfectly neat garden with its artificial grass. "Where will you find some?"

"I know just the place." Lottie raced home and collected a handful of small slugs from the bug hotel.

Then, she laid them in a trail from the hedgehog in the golf hole to the gap under the fence leading to her garden.

They all watched as the hedgehog began to uncurl.

"Look at its tiny nose and ears," Petunia said excitedly. "Oooh, now I can see its nose whiffling! It's got whiskers!"

Lottie couldn't wait to draw a picture of it in her nature notebook. It looked so cute!

She watched in awe as the
hedgehog got to its feet and scurried
to the closest slug. It patted it with its
paws until the slug shrank into a ball.
The hedgehog gobbled it up.

"Yum!" Noah said, wrinkling his nose.

"It's loving its dinner," Lottie laughed, as the hedgehog moved on to the next slug and the next.

"Your plan seems to have worked, Lottie." Noah's dad breathed a sigh of relief as the hedgehog squeezed under the gap in the fence. He turned to Petunia. "Shall we finish our golf?"

"Let's call it a draw," Petunia said. "It's been a lovely night, but I should be getting home."

Suddenly she jumped and gasped, "There's something on my neck!"

"And mine!" Mr Parfitt exclaimed.

"It must be a hedgehog flea . . . Oh, no, wait a minute, it's a moth . . . "

"Yikes!" they both yelled together.

"They're a perfect match!" Noah laughed.

"They are!" Lottie agreed. "Now, let's get back to my garden and see what the hedgehog's doing."

They let themselves in the back gate and hurried up the path.

"Don't step on that huge slug," Noah warned.

"That's not a slug," she laughed. "That's Nacho's banana skin."

But before she could pick it up, Mrs Boffin opened the kitchen door. Einstein squeezed out into the garden and sniffed suspiciously at it.

"How's the apple sauce going?" Lottie asked her.

"Slowly," said Mum. "The apples were all over the garage floor and I had to pick them up one by one. Al's in big trouble. He must have used the old crate for one of his experiments. He didn't even ask . . ."

For a moment Lottie was tempted to let her twin brother take the blame, but that wasn't very fair. "Um, Mum, it was me . . . " Lottie began to explain.

"Precious! Stop!" There was a yell from the Goods' garden.

Lottie glanced towards the bottom of the fence between the Boffins' garden and the Goods'. She could see a nose and whiskers. Mrs Good's cat was attempting to squeeze through the hole that she'd made for the hedgehog. Fortunately Einstein hadn't noticed.

"Don't worry, Precious is too big to get through the gap," Lottie called.

"And exactly why is there a hole under my fence?" Mrs Good thundered.

"Er . . . It's just a tiny space for a hedgehog to get through," Lottie called. "They need to roam."

"A hedgehog?" Mrs Good sounded outraged. "Precious might catch fleas or get prickled!"

"Hedgehogs do have prickles, but they rarely have fleas," Lottie tried to explain as Precious' nose disappeared from under the fence.

But Mrs Good crooned, "Come to your

mumsy, darling! Mumsy won't let that hedgehog prickle you. I think we'd better go and have a little talk with Lottie and her mother, don't you?"

"Oh no!" Lottie and Mrs Boffin groaned. Noah looked puzzled.

"She's always coming round to complain," Lottie explained. "But it's usually about Al and his experiments."

She reluctantly opened the back gate. Mrs Good was standing there frowning with Precious cradled in her arms.

"Where's that dog of yours? Is it safe to come in?" Mrs Good asked.

"Einstein won't chase Precious if you keep holding her," Lottie reassured her.

Mrs Good followed Lottie to the Boffins' kitchen door.

"Mind the banana— " Lottie began.

Too late. Mrs Good stepped on Nacho's banana skin. Precious leaped from her arms as she steadied herself against the door jamb.

WOOF! Einstein bounded up. Precious shot off.

"Precious!" Mrs Good called. "Come back to Mumsy!"

"Look! She's found the hedgehog!" Noah commented.

At the back of the garden, Precious was staring curiously at a small, round prickly ball.

"Don't touch it, Precious! You might get a nasty surprise!" Mrs Good raced over and scooped her cat into her arms. Precious wriggled and squirmed as she was carried away.

Lottie grabbed Einstein's collar and they all watched from a distance as the hedgehog slowly uncurled, whiffled its whiskers, and shuffled happily towards the pile of leaves that concealed the hedgehog shelter.

"It'll be safe in there!" Lottie breathed a sigh of relief. She smiled at Mrs Good. "If you leave the hole under the fence, the hedgehog will come into your garden and eat lots of your slugs before it hibernates. It's found the shelter I built.

"I hope it'll hibernate here, and come out and eat more slugs in the spring!"

"That would be good for my hostas," Mrs Good murmured thoughtfully as the hedgehog pushed its nose into the leaves. "Maybe we should keep the hole after all. And it is quite cute, isn't it, Precious?

MIAOW! Precious twisted in her arms and dropped to the ground.

She raced up to the disappearing hedgehog and stretched out a paw as if she was going to pat its spiny bottom. *Oh no!* thought Lottie, but the hedgehog didn't seem worried at all.

"Precious, no!" squealed Mrs Good.

"Precious!" Nacho squawked, imitating her voice perfectly. "Precious! Precious!"

WOOF! WOOF! WOOF! barked Einstein.

Precious gave a little mew of alarm, turned tail, and launched herself back into Mrs Good's arms.

"My poor, frightened kitty," Mrs Good crooned. "Don't worry. Mumsy will tell everyone off for making all that terrible noise and frightening you." She glared at everyone.

"Ummm, please excuse me, I need to check on the apple sauce." Mrs Boffin disappeared into the kitchen.

"And I should get back home, to . . . er, check if I can still see Mars," said Noah. He lowered his voice. "What's your excuse, Lottie?"

Lottie glanced at the thunderous frown on Mrs Good's face. "I'm so sorry

Precious is upset," she said, "but I have to get the pets inside, check on the hedgehog, and finish off my nature notebook so I can send it in to Samira!"

"You mean Samira Breeze on 'Every Little Thing'?" Mrs Good's frown cleared. "We love that show!"

"Do you?" Lottie gasped.

"Oh yes." A smile crept over Mrs Good's stern face. "Precious loves watching programmes about wildlife."

"Me too." Lottie's eyes shone. "I love nature, don't you?"

COOL FACTS ABOUT NIGHT CREATURES

Animals that come out at night to hunt for food are called nocturnal animals. Their senses are adapted to help them live in the dark.

Owls have huge eyes with big pupils that help them see in the dark.

A fox's hearing is so good they can hear moles digging underground.

Badgers have poor eyesight, but an excellent sense of smell and great hearing. They love worms!

Cats like Precious have special eyes that adapt quickly from light to dark.

MY COMPOST HEAP

EVERY
LITTLE THING
MATTERS

Hedgehogs love to eat worms! Worms often come up to the surface at night, especially if it has rained. I'm making the soil better for worms and plants by making a compost heap.

Shredded paper

Grass cuttings

Vegetable peel, eggshells, coffee grounds, and tea bags (as long as they don't contain plastic).

Dead leaves

Sticks

I used some old bricks as a base. You can use an old crate or bin as a container. Or just make a heap.

DON'T PUT IN!
Cooked food scraps, meat or bones, weeds.

I let it sit for three months, then carefully turned the heap with a garden fork.

When it's dark and crumbly, your compost is ready to dig into your soil.

Samira says you can easily make gardens more friendly for night creatures.

I'm helping every little thing that visits my garden at night by making sure that they have water, food and shelter.

Flowers like jasmine, honeysuckle and evening primrose release their scent in the evening and attract moths.

Nocturnal animals are shy and very hard to spot! It's best to sit in the dark and wait quietly for them. Don't shine a torch on them, or they will run away!

SAMIRA'S CONSERVATION CORNER

Are you helping to protect nature in your garden or neighbourhood, like Lottie? Then you're a conservationist. All over the world, conservationists are working hard to prevent species from becoming extinct.

EVERY LITTLE THING MATTERS

♡ WHAT YOU CAN DO: ♡

Everything in nature is connected so it's important to help save all plants and animals!

Samira

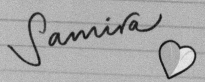

Like hedgehogs, porcupines and echidnas (spiny anteaters) also have spines.

Echidnas are living examples of the primitive mammals called monotremes that evolved at time of dinosaurs. They lay eggs, which they incubate and hatch in their pouch.

Short-beaked echidna

Long-beaked echidna

Like hedgehogs, they are mostly nocturnal.

The long-beaked echidna (native to New Guinea) is critically endangered. Conservationists are setting up refuges to help save them.

IT'S ALWAYS WILD WITH LOTTIE ABOUT!